KB108181

녹두
장군

녹두장군

발행일	2020년 9월 11일
지은이	엄정옥
펴낸이	손형국
펴낸곳	(주)북랩
편집인	선일영
편집	정두철, 윤성아, 최승헌, 이예지, 최예원
디자인	이현수, 한수희, 김민하, 김윤주, 허지혜
제작	박기성, 황동현, 구성우, 권태련
마케팅	김회란, 박진관, 장은별
출판등록	2004. 12. 1(제2012-000051호)
주소	서울특별시 금천구 가산디지털 1로 168, 우림라이온스밸리 B동 B113~114호, C동 B101호
홈페이지	www.book.co.kr
전화번호	(02)2026-5777
팩스	(02)2026-5747

ISBN   979-11-6539-366-3 03810 (종이책)   979-11-6539-367-0 05810 (전자책)

이 도서의 국립중앙도서관 출판예정도서목록(CIP)은 서지정보유통지원시스템 홈페이지(http://seoji.nl.go.kr)와
국가자료공동목록시스템(http://www.nl.go.kr/kolisnet)에서 이용하실 수 있습니다.
(CIP제어번호: 2020038608)

(주)북랩 성공출판의 파트너

북랩 홈페이지와 패밀리 사이트에서 다양한 출판 솔루션을 만나 보세요!

홈페이지 book.co.kr   •   **블로그** blog.naver.com/essaybook   •   **출판문의** book@book.co.kr

녹두장군

General Nokdu

엄정옥 시집

북랩 book Lab

시인의 말

　하이쿠는 5, 7, 5의 음수율을 지닌 17자로 된 일본의 짧은 정형시다. 여기에 계어(季語)와 기레지가 반드시 있어야 한다.

　계어(季語)는 계절을 상징하는 시어를 의미한다. 기레지는 매듭을 지으면서 어느 한 단락에서 끊어줌으로써 강한 영탄이나 여운을 줄 때 사용하는 표현을 지칭한다.

　하이쿠는 세계에서 가장 짧은 시 형태로 유명하다.

　서구에는 잘 소개되어 있으나 우리나라에는 거의 알려져 있지 않다.

이런 점을 감안하여 필자는 한국적 정서를 반영하고 5, 7, 5의 음수율은 지키되 계어와 기레지의 사용에서 자유로운(계어와 기레지를 사용할 수도 있고, 사용하지 않을 수도 있다) 시를 썼다. 이 새로운 시형을 한국적 하이쿠(K-하이쿠)라고 명명해도 좋지 않을까 하고 제안해 본다.

　한국적 하이쿠의 세계화를 위해서 본서는 영어로 번역됐으며 번역은 공군사관학교 교수였던 엄윤종 교수가 맡았다.

이 시집을 통해서 내외국인들의 한국적 하이쿠 이해와 영어 학습에 도움이 되었으면 하는 바람이다.

2020년 8월

문학박사, 시인 김정옥

목차

제1부

세월 *Time*

황혼

인생의 황혼
노을에 붉게 물든
찬란한 슬픔

Twilight

The twilight of life
The twilight reddened by dusk
The brilliant sorrow

세월

흐르는 세월
두 손으로 막아도
어쩔 수 없네

Time

Time flies
We only try to prevent it
We only try⋯

단풍

내장산 단풍
그대는 어이하여
붉기만 한가

Maple

The maple of Nai Zang mountain
I only wonder reason
Why it is so red

풍등

사월의 풍등
하늘까지 올라가
빛을 밝히네

Wind Lantern

The wind lantern of April
Shot up to the sky
Brighten the light

생명 소리

그대 듣는가
수액의 옹알이를
생명 소리를

Sound of Life

Do you hear the sound of life?
The murmur of the tree sap
The sound of life

신록

5월의 신록
계절의 여왕이여
생명의 약동

Fresh Verdure

The fresh verdure of May
The Queen of the season
The lively motion of life

낙조

불타는 낙조
그대는 어이하여
타오르는가

Glow of Setting Sun

The burning glow of the setting sun
What is the reason that you burn?

연등 1

연등은 등대
캄캄한 어둠에서
빛을 밝히네

Lotus Lantern 1

The lotus lantern is the lighthouse
It brightens the light in the darkness

매미

여름 매미여
노래가 우렁차다
최고의 절정

Cicada

The cicada of summer
You sing a sonorous song
You reach the zenith

보리밭

보리밭에서
뉘 부르는 소리가
울려 퍼진다

Barley Field

In the barley field
A song which calls someone
Rang far away

사월의 노래

사월의 노래
목련꽃 그늘에서
울려 퍼지네

Song of April

A song of April is rung vigorously
Under the shadow of magnolia blossom

연등 2

연등은 연꽃
부처님 오신 날에
불을 밝히네

Lotus Lantern 2

The lotus lantern is the lotus flower
The lotus lantern will be brightened
On the Buddhist day

가을

가을은 단풍
메이플시럽처럼
가을은 달다

Autumn

The autumn is the maple
Like the maple syrup
The autumn is sweet

만월

추석은 만월
달이 차면 기운다
인생의 공전

Full Moon

The Korean Thanksgiving Day is full moon
The full moon wanes when it is full
The revolution of life

만추晚秋

늦은 가을에
〈만추〉가 생각나는
러브 스토리

Late Autumn

In the late autumn
Movie "Late Autumn" reminds me
The love story

연

연날리기다
하늘을 날아간다
동심의 회귀

Kite

Let's fly the kite
The kite flies to the sky
Return to the mind of child

개나리

봄의 전령사
개나리가 피었다
노란 병아리

Forsythia

The forsythia blooms
The messenger of spring
The forsythia is the yellow chick

연꽃

연꽃의 축제
부처님의 꽃이다
연꽃은 연등

Lotus Flower

The festival of lotus flower
The lotus flower is the flower of Buddha
The lotus flower is the lotus lantern

동백꽃

겨울의 동백
동백꽃이 붉다네
동백꽃 연정

Camellia Flower

The winter camellia
The camellia flower is red
The ardent love of camellia flower

국화꽃

가을의 국화
나의 누님 같은 꽃
국화꽃 향기

Chrysanthemum

The chrysanthemum of Autumn
The chrysanthemum is like my elder sister
The fragrance of chrysanthemum

살구꽃

봄은 살구꽃
마음의 봄 살구꽃
분홍 살구꽃

Apricot Blossom

The spring is the apricot blossom
The apricot blossom is the spring of mind
The pink apricot blossom

수박

시원한 수박
수박은 하모니카
불면증 예방

Watermelon

The cool watermelon
The watermelon is harmonica
The prevention of insomnia

청포도

청포도 사랑
사랑이 주렁주렁
청포도 연가

Green Grape

The love toward the green grape
The cluster of the love
The love song of the green grape

복사꽃

복사꽃 고향
고향이 그립다네
복사꽃 사랑

Peach Blossom

The hometown of the peach blossom
The homesick
The love of the peach blossom

홍시

홍시는 엄마
엄마가 그립다네
홍시는 달다

Ripe Persimmon

The ripe persimmon is mother
I miss my mother so much
The ripe persimmon is sweet

제2부

무지개 *Rainbow*

봄

청춘의 봄 봄
가슴이 두근두근
봄은 무지개

Spring

The wonderful spring of youth
The mind is pulsing
The spring is the rainbow

달

달아 밝은 달
이태백이 놀던 달
달마중 가자

Moon

Hi moon, the bright moon
The moon that Lee Tae Baik* plays
Let's go to meet the moon

---

*   Lee Tae Baik: The famous Chinese poet.

모과 예찬

모과 예쁘다
모과도 과일인가
최고다 모과

Adoration of Chinese Quince

Chinese quince is fine
Is Chinese quince one of fruits?
Chinese quince is best

진달래

사랑의 희열
진달래 피고 지고
봄날은 간다

Azalea

The ecstasy of love
The azalea blooms and falls
The spring has gone

메밀꽃

메밀꽃 피다
한여름 밤의 눈꽃
메밀꽃 축제

Buckwheat Flower

The buckwheat flower blossoms
The snow flower of midsummer night
The festival of snow

귀뚜라미

귀뚜라미다
가을의 전령사여
청아한 선율

Cricket

It is cricket
A messenger of the autumn
Elegant melody

눈

눈이 내린다
크리스마스 전야
징글벨이다

Snow

It snows
It is Christmas Eve
We hear jingle bell

고추

한국의 고추
고추 매운맛 볼래?
청양고추다

Korean Red Pepper

The red pepper of Korea
Do you want to taste the hot pepper?
It is Chung Yang red pepper

벚꽃

화사한 계절
벚꽃이 만개했다
벚꽃 축제다

Cherry Blossom

The splendor season
The cherry blossom is in full bloom
The festival of cherry blossom

연어

모천母川이 좋다
고향으로 돌아온
연어의 회귀

Salmon

The salmon likes its mother river
It comes back to its hometown
Return of salmon

녹두장군

동학농민군
녹두장군 전봉준
파랑새 전설

General Nokdu

The peasant soldiers of Donghak
General Nokdu Jeon Bong-jun
The legend of the blue bird

이팝꽃 1

5월의 눈꽃
여름 크리스마스
영원한 사랑

Lee Pap Flower 1

The snow flower of May
The summer Christmas
The eternal love

오동잎

오동잎 지다
만추晩秋의 전령사
우수憂愁의 시작

Paulownia Leaf

The paulownia leaf falls
It is the messenger of the late autumn
The beginning of melancholy

삼계탕

복날의 음식
최고 보양식이다
순 우리 음식

Boiled Chicken Soup *(Samgye-tang)*

The food of midsummer
It increases your stamina
The food origin from Korea

성묘

추석의 성묘
조상님 챙기는 날
전래의 전통

Visit to Our Ancestor's Grave

A visit to our ancestor's grave
On Korean Thanksgiving Day
The visiting day to our ancestor's grave
The old tradition of Korea

가을

풀벌레 소리
가을의 전령사다
우수의 계절

Autumn

The song of the grass insects
It is the messenger of the autumn
The season of melancholy

파도

여름의 파도
파도여 물결쳐라
격랑의 파도

Waves

The waves of summer
Oh! fluctuate as you can, waves
The raging waves

봉숭아

봉선화 계절
봉숭아 물들이는
여인네 연정

Balsamine

The season of balsamine
Women dye their nails with it
The ardent love of women

무화과

금단의 열매
에덴에서 추방된
아담과 이브

Fig

The forbidden fruit
Banished from the paradise
Adam and Eve

용눈이오름

한라산 오름
야생화 지천이다
야생화 천국

Dragon Eye's Ascent

The ascent of Han Ra mountain
Home of wild flowers
The paradise of wild flowers

비닐

비닐 반 생명
생명이 지고 나는
순환의 반역

Vinyl

The vinyl is anti-life
The cycle of life
Vinyl rejects the cycle

비핵화

핵은 반 생명
비핵화 생명의 길
공존의 길이다

Denuclearization

The nucleus is anti-life
The denuclearization is the way of life
The way of co-existence

웹

웹은 거미줄
정보화 사회 총아
정보의 고리

Web

The web is the spider's thread
The darling of information era
The chain of information

무지개

아름다운 꿈
이상향理想鄉으로 비약飛躍
멋진 신세계

Rainbow

The beautiful dream
A leap to an ideal world
The brave new world

제3부
문주란文珠蘭, *Crinum*

2020.
권실

약사여래藥師如來

약사여래藥師如來*는
새로운 구원자다
질병의 퇴치

Bhechadjaguru

Bhechadjaguru is a new Salvationist
The subjugation of disease

---

* 약사여래: 중생의 질병을 고쳐주는 약사신앙의 대상이 되는 보살.

나팔꽃

기쁜 소식이
임으로부터 올까?
나팔꽃 연정

Morning Glory

May the pleasant news come
From my sweetheart?
The love of morning glory

석류

석류의 계절
에스트로겐 풍부
여성의 과일

Pomegranate

The season of pomegranate
A pomegranate has rich estrogen
The fruit of woman

대나무

대나무 단심丹心
정몽주의 〈단심가〉
대나무 절개

Bamboo

The fidelity of bamboo
The fidelity song of Jeong Mong-ju
The loyalty of bamboo

도道

도는 길이다
둘이 하나 되는 길
참 생명의 길

Tao

Tao is the road
The way that two becomes one
The road of true life

기계

문명의 총아
동일한 동작 반복
기술의 시대

Machine

A darling of civilization
The repetition of the same motion
The time of technique

컴퓨터

사이버 세상
무소불위無所不爲의 능력
디지털 시대

Computer

The cyber-world
Unlimited capability
The digital age

태극

태극은 일자一者
만물의 근원이다
태극이 도道다

Great Absolute

Great Absolute is one letter
Source of all things in the universe
Great Absolute is Tao

사랑

완벽한 사랑
정신 육체의 조화
이상적 사랑

Love

The perfect love
The harmony of spirit and flesh
The ideal love

제비

돌아온 제비
복을 얼마나 줄까?
물 찬 제비다

Swallow

The returning of swallow
What kind of fortune will you bring?
The splendid swallow

문주란文珠蘭

제주 토끼섬
꽃대 말자지 같은
천연기념물

Crinum

The rabbit island of Je Ju
A long flower stalk that Looks alike horse's penis
The natural monument

죽음

삶의 끝 아닌
새로운 삶의 시작
생명의 순환

Death

The death is not the end of life
But the new beginning of life
The circulation of life

자연

공생의 원칙
균형과 조화 이룸
자연의 조화

Nature

The principle of co-existence
The accomplishment of balance and harmony
The harmony of nature

공생

양쪽에 이익
더불어 사는 지혜
상리相利 공생共生*임

Co-Existence

Mutual benefits
The knowledge to live together
The co-existence of giving
Interests to everybody

---

* 상리 공생: 모두에게 이익을 주다.

코카콜라

코카콜라병
완벽 여인의 허리
페로몬* 자극

Coca-Cola

The bottle of Coca-Cola
The loin of the perfect lady
The impetus of pheromone

---

* 페로몬: 동물이 같은 종의 이성異性을 유인하는 물질.

낙엽

가을의 전령
낙엽이 떨어지다
쓸쓸한 가을

Fallen Leaves

The messenger of the autumn
The leaves fall
The lonesome autumn

나미브 고목

나미브 고목
생명이 없는 나무
600년의 세월

Dead Tree of Namib Desert

The dead tree of Namib Desert
A lifeless tree
Time of six hundred years

윤회

탄생과 죽음
삶의 수레바퀴다
생명의 고리

Samsara(Metempsychosis)

The birth and the death
The wheel of the life
The ring of the life

각覺

불자佛子 깨달음
세계의 실제 모습
실상實相을 아는 것

Awakening

Awakening of Buddhist
The real aspect of the world
Awakening is to attain the spiritual illumination

니르바나

괴로움의 멸滅
완전한 해탈 경지
불성佛性을 얻음

Nirvana

The disappearance of affliction
The state of the perfect Buddhistic emancipation
Full gain of nature of Buddha

반야바라밀다

완전한 지혜
집착하지 않는 것
공空의 세계다

Praina-Paramita

The perfect wisdom
The Stoic life
All is vanity

가을바람

바람이 분다
허가 없이 온 바람
가을이 깊다

Autumn Wind

The wind blows in the autumn
The wind without permission
The autumn becomes deeper

곶감

인생은 곶감
곶감 빼 먹듯 한다
곶감은 달다

Dried Persimmon

The life is a dried persimmon
We eat away it from our savings
A dried persimmon is sweet

가을 들판

가을 들판에
황금물결이 인다
가을은 황금

Autumn Field

In the autumn field
The golden waves move in the waves
The autumn is the gold

참게

참게의 계절
참게 매운탕 최고
게 맛을 아나?

Korean Crab

The season of Korean crab
The taste of Korean crab, the best
Do you know the taste?

제4부

동지冬至, *Winter Solstice*

순례

순례 떠나다
산티아고 순례길
마음의 희열

Pilgrimage

I go to pilgrimage
Camino de Santiago
The delight of the mind

고드름

고드름 세상
처마마다 고드름
겨울이 깊다

Icicle

The world of an icicle
Icicles hang on the eaves
The winter becomes deeper

얼음

투명한 유리
마음 비추는 거울
겨울의 첨병

Ice

The transparent plain glass
The mirror that reflects the mind
The advance guard of winter

동천冬天

겨울의 하늘
하늘 나는 기러기
겨울은 춥다

Wintry Sky

The sky of winter
A wild goose that flies the sky
The winter is very cold

소통

경험과 경청
말을 잘 듣는 능력
공감의 세계

Communication

Experience and listening
The ability to listen
The world of sympathy

원圓

원圓은 둥글다
인생은 순환한다
우리 삶은 원圓

Circle

The circle is round
The life is the circulation
Our life is like the circle

반딧불이

청정淸淨의 상징
사랑의 빛 반딧불
무주 구천동

Firefly

The symbol of purity
A firefly is the light of love
Mu Ju Guchondong

오늘

절대적인 날
오늘이 영원이다
오늘은 오늘

Today

Today is the absolute day
Today is the eternity
Today is today

모른다

숭산 가르침
오직 모를 뿐이다
공空의 깨달음

I Don't Know

The teaching of Buddhist monk Soongsan
I only don't know
The awakening of vanity

자목련

자줏빛 목련
슬픈 이야기의 꽃
나무의 연꽃

Lily Magnolia

A purple magnolia
The flower of sad story
The lotus flower of the tree

초록 생명 예찬

초록 엽록소
초록은 산소 배출
초록은 생명

Praise of Green Life

The green chlorophyll
The green discharges the oxygen
The green is the life

크리스마스 캐럴

찰스 디킨스
구두쇠 스크루지
천사로 변신

A Christmas Carol

Charles Dickens' novel
A Christmas Carol'hero is Scrooge
He was a miser
Scrooge became an angel on Christmas Eve

긍정의 힘

고맙습니다
긍정적 사고방식
행복의 원천

Power of Affirmation

Thank you
The affirmative way of thinking
The source of happiness

진안 마이산

말 귀 생김새
암수 마이산이네
음양의 조화

Jinan Maisan

The shape of horse's ear
There are female Maisan and male Maisan
The harmony of Yin and Yang

명상瞑想

나에게 집중
여기로 돌아오기
마음의 회복

Meditation

The concentration on me
The returning to this place
The recovery of the mind

칡의 변신

숲 파괴 주범
친환경 천연섬유
칡 섬유 개발

Change of Arrowroot

The principal destroyer of the forest
The natural fiber of the pro-environment
The development of the arrowroot fiber

무궁화

끝없이 핀다
인내 끈기 진취성
우리 국화國花다

Rose of Sharon(Mugunghwa)

Mugunghwa blossomed endlessly
Patience, tenacity, and progressiveness
The national flower of Korea

동지冬至

동지冬至는 팥죽
동치미와 함께 먹는
팥죽의 묘미

Winter Solstice

The winter solstice is the red bean porridge
We eat it with the watery radish Kimchi
The nicety of the red bean porridge

겨울 동치미

콜라보다도
시원한 우리 음식
겨울의 별미

Watery Radish Kimchi of Winter

It is Korea's native food and
Cooler than Coca-Cola
The delicate taste of winter

설

고유의 명절
설날 새 옷 입는다
민족 대이동

Lunar New Year's Day

Korea's festive day
We put on the new dress on this day
The great movement of people

유채꽃

유채꽃 피다
노란 병아리 떼
유채밭 향기

Rape Flower

A rape flower blossoms
Flocks of yellow chicken
The fragrance of the rape field

불나방

치열한 욕망
타오르는 불꽃
죽음과 파멸

Tiger Moth

The intensified desire
The blazing flame
The death and the destruction

결혼반지

결혼의 서약
평생 사랑의 증표
마음의 희열

Wedding Ring

The pledge of marriage
A voucher of the everlasting love
The delight of mind

개밥바라기*

하늘에 뜬 별
개밥바라기 뜨면
개밥 줘야 해

Venus

The star in the sky
When Venus comes out
We must give the dog's food

---

* 개밥바라기: 금성Venus.